A JIGSAW JONES MYSTERY®

The Case of the
Food Fight

Read all the Jigsaw Jones Mysteries!

The Case of the
Food Fight

by James Preller
illustrated by Jamie Smith
cover illustration by R. W. Alley

A
LITTLE APPLE
PAPERBACK

SCHOLASTIC INC.
New York   Toronto   London   Auckland   Sydney
Mexico City   New Delhi   Hong Kong   Buenos Aires

ISBN 0-439-67807-2

12 11 10 9 8 7 6   8 9 10/0

Printed in the U.S.A.   40
First printing, September 2005

This book is dedicated to Hostess Cupcakes.

*With special thanks to Ellen Mosher,
second-grade teacher at
Westmere Elementary.*
—JP

CONTENTS

Chapter One

Hiding from Dad

Okay. So there I was. Bothering nobody. Lying on the floor of my bedroom, doing a jigsaw puzzle. It was a brain-buster. Five hundred pieces of the African plains. Lions and elephants and zebras.

Plus lots and lots of yellow grass. It was making me bug-eyed.

But I can't walk away from a puzzle. Once I start, I stick around until I finish it. Sure, sometimes I have to eat dinner. Sometimes I have to go to the bathroom. But I always come back. I have to get every piece in

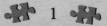 1

place. All neat and tidy. I can't explain why. I'm just built that way.

So like I said, I'm bothering nobody. When suddenly, my brothers, Daniel and Nick, burst through the bedroom door.

"Dad's home!" Nick cried.

"Hide!" Daniel advised.

"Huh?"

Nick stopped. The dirty rat stood on top of my puzzle. "Dad went food shopping! He'll want help carrying the bags!"

Then Nick turned, sending puzzle pieces flying across the floor. "Quick, Jigsaw," he urged. "In here."

"Now!" Daniel screamed.

So I jumped into the closet with them. Nick slammed the door closed.

On my nose.

Ouch.

It's not easy being the youngest in the family.

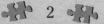

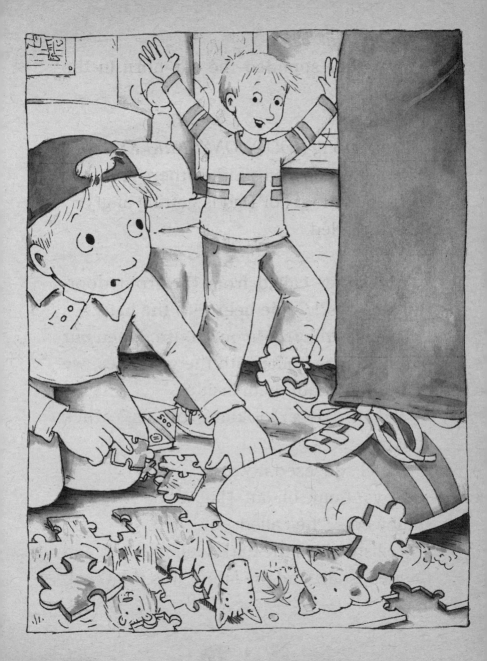

Honk! Honk!

My father sounded the car horn in the driveway.

Silence.

Then a long *HOOOOONNNNKKKKK!*

Daniel whispered, "Either there's a giant goose outside . . . or Dad is getting angry."

Nick giggled.

"*Shhh.*"

My father called from the front door, "Boys? Boys?! Come help with the bags."

That was the rule in our house. When our parents came home with the groceries, we had to help haul them inside.

"*Shhhh.* He's looking for us," Nick whispered.

Daniel squeezed my arm.

"Boys? Come on out. I know you're hiding somewhere!" he called.

We listened in the dark. I felt like Jack and the Beanstalk, and my father was the Giant.

Wham! Dad threw open the bathroom door.

Whoosh. He slid back the shower curtain.

Stomp, stomp, crash. He banged around in different bedrooms.

Fee-fi-fo-fum!

"That leaves Jigsaw's room," he said aloud.

Woof, woof! That was my dog, Rags. He was giving us away.

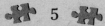

"They aren't under the bed," he murmured.

The Giant was getting closer.

Daniel, Nick, and I huddled together in one giant bear hug.

"Hmmm?" my father said. "Why are you sniffing at the closet door, Rags?"

And closer.

Yipes. The jig was up.

"AHA!"

My father pulled open the closet door. Out we tumbled, spilling onto the floor. Giggling and happy.

"Nice try, boys," he said. "Now bring in those bags or *no food* for you!"

Usually, my mom is the one who goes shopping. But she was away for a couple of days, visiting Aunt Harriet. My mom buys healthy things, food that is good for us. If that sounds boring, you should try eating it. But sometimes my dad shops. He buys stuff that my mother would never touch.

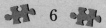

Dad, you see, has a sweet tooth.

A big one.

We might not have liked carrying the heavy bags, but we liked checking out all the tasty treats.

"Wow," Nick exclaimed. "This cereal is totally awesome. It's mini chocolate chip cookies . . ."

". . . that are *frosted* with sugar!" Daniel exclaimed.

"And they come with rainbow-colored marshmallows!" I cheered.

"Hey, look at this," Daniel gushed. "A whole bag of Snickers bars!"

"That stuff's expensive," my father said. "So take it easy, boys. Prices are going through the roof."

"Sure, Dad, whatever," Nick said. "Now let's chow down on some of this junk food before Mom gets back from her trip."

Chapter Two

Carrots & Cupcakes

I checked my lunch box as soon as I got to my classroom on Monday morning. Yes, it was still there. A double-stuffed fudge cupcake topped with peanut butter morsels.

Life was good.

Especially when Dad packed the desserts.

Every kid knows: There are two important parts to every school day. Lunch and recess. Everything else is filler.

"That cupcake looks good," admired

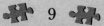

Helen Zuckerman. She shoved her backpack into a cubby.

"Yeah," I answered. "It's topped with creamy peanut butter morsels."

"I wish my mother packed junk food. I get baby carrots for dessert," Helen sighed.

"Ha-ha, carrots!" scoffed Bobby Solofsky. "I got a bag of jelly beans!"

"Jelly beans rot your teeth," Helen replied. "And besides, carrots are good for me."

Solofsky slid his tongue across his teeth. He made a sucking sound. "Carrots don't really make you see any better," he claimed.

"Do so."

"Do not," Solofsky replied. "That's just something parents say to make you eat 'em."

"I don't believe you," Helen said. "Carrots help you see in the dark!" She was getting annoyed.

"Not true," Solofsky said. "Think about it. Imagine if you ate carrots all day long . . . for like four weeks in a row. . . ."

"Just carrots?" I asked.

"Just carrots," Solofsky answered.

"I'd turn orange," Helen groaned.

Solofsky continued, "If a couple of carrots are supposed to help you see better, then what if you ate *thousands* of carrots? It ought to give you superpower vision."

"Like Superman's X-ray eyes," Stringbean Noonan murmured.

I looked around. Some kids had gathered around our conversation. When it came to superpowers, everybody had an opinion.

"If you ate tons of carrots," Solofsky reasoned, "you should be able to burn holes through walls with laser-beam eyeballs."

Helen frowned. "That's silly."

"That's cool," Danika Starling said. "It would soooo rock to have X-ray vision!"

"I'd rather fly," said Kim Lewis. "What

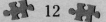

about you guys? What superpower would you pick?"

"I'd want superstrength," decided Bigs Maloney.

(This was like a pillow wishing it was soft. Bigs already had superstrength.)

"Invisibility," I decided. "I could spy on people."

"I'd want everything that I touch to turn into pizza," Joey Pignattano said. Typical Joey. Food was all he ever thought about. If

food were math, Joey would be a rocket scientist.

"What about the power to walk through walls?" Eddie Becker suggested.

Helen frowned. "That sounds gross. All that plaster would make me sneeze. What if you got stuck in there?"

"No way, Helen," Bobby said. "You are not going to get stuck. It's a superpower!"

Helen balled her hand into a fist. She muttered darkly.

Clearly, Helen had an anger management problem.

Kim Lewis clucked, "I'd rather fly."

"Flying would be *sweet*," Eddie Becker said. "But it's got to be boring up there. Just you and empty sky. All the action is down here on earth."

We argued for a few more minutes. Helen was getting madder and madder at Solofsky. Then Ms. Gleason clapped her hands.

Clap-clap.

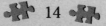 14

That was our signal. We clapped back, *clap-clap-clap*. We quickly took our seats, ready to begin the day.

I heard Solofsky whisper to Helen, "We'll finish this at lunch."

Now all we had to do was kill time until lunch.

Ms. Gleason sure kept us busy. It was a gym day, so school was actually pretty good. Finally, it was time for lunch. As we headed out the door, Ms. Gleason called my name. "Jigsaw, please deliver these papers to Mr. Alonzo. You can catch up with everyone in the cafeteria." That was fine by me. I love special errands.

Good thing it didn't take long.

I might have missed the food fight.

Chapter Three

Food Fight!

THHHHHWAPP!

The moment I walked into the cafeteria, something hit me in the face.

Something wet.

Something squishy.

Something green.

Something . . . yummy. *Mmm.* Jell-O.

"FOOD FIGHT!" a chorus of voices cried.

After that, the next few seconds were a blur.

Meatballs bounced. Green Jell-O smashed. Spaghetti flew. Mashed potatoes splattered.

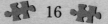

Kids dived under tables. Some kids hurled fistfuls of food like snowballs. Others squealed like pigs and, to be honest, acted like pigs, too. Wilbur, Babe, Porky, and Miss Piggy had nothing on us. *Oink, oink.*

I even heard somebody bark. *Yip-yip-yap!*

Boys and girls screamed and laughed. The lunch aides screamed louder. But they weren't laughing. Soon, it was all over.

Wow, my first food fight. It was the most exciting thing I had ever seen. But now I looked around. I felt my stomach sink. We were in big trouble.

Mrs. Minaya, a lunch aide, was standing on a chair. The veins popped out of her neck. She looked really mad. Mashed potato dripped from her dress. *Plip, plip, plop.*

The other lunch aide, Mrs. Randolph, swooped across the room toward Joey Pignattano. "He's the one!" she screeched. "He's the one who started it!"

Mrs. Randolph led Joey out the door by

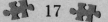 17

the elbow. Joey's eyes were wide and bulging. He wore a look of absolute terror, like a field mouse caught in the talons of a hawk. As he passed me, Joey reached for my arm. "Jigsaw, you've got to help me," he pleaded. "I'm innocent!"

Teachers filed into the cafeteria. Each one looked upset and angry. The cafeteria ladies stood with their hands on their hips. Then came poor Mr. Copabianco, the janitor. He stopped at the doorway and looked around the room. He didn't look mad. No, it was worse than that. He looked *disappointed.* By us. His friends.

He left and soon returned with a mop, a bucket, and cleaning supplies.

"No," Ms. Gleason said to him. "This isn't your job, Mr. Copabianco. The children will clean up the mess," she ordered.

I found a spot next to Mila Yeh. She is my best friend, my classmate, and my partner.

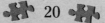

We are detectives together. For a dollar a day, we make problems go away.

But right now, we were scrubbing the floor . . . trying to make spaghetti sauce go away.

"What happened?" I whispered.

Mila shrugged. "I don't know. All of a sudden, food was flying. I ducked under a table."

"Joey says he's innocent," I told her.

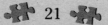

Suddenly, two feet stood in front of us. The feet were attached to the skinny legs of Mrs. Randolph. She squinted at us through small dark eyes.

"Silence," she hissed.

We put our heads down and scrubbed.

A moment later Mila whispered, "You better go wash up, Jigsaw. You've got Jell-O in your hair."

Chapter Four

In the Boys' Room

The boys' bathroom was buzzing. Everybody was washing their hands and faces. Ralphie Jordan picked meatballs out of his ears.

"I got nailed in the back by a slice of pizza," Eddie Becker said.

"I don't know who I hit," Solofsky bragged. "I just grabbed a handful of mashed potatoes and fired!"

Bigs Maloney stood at the sink. He frowned at his shirt. Once upon a time, it had been white and clean. Now it looked

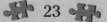 23

like, well, it had been in a food fight. "I feel gross," Bigs muttered.

"You don't look so hot, either," I observed.

Bigs scowled at me in the mirror.

I turned to a group of guys. "So who started it?" I asked.

No one heard me.

I asked louder: "WHO STARTED IT?"

No one spoke. A few boys shrugged. Some looked at the floor, others glanced at Bigs Maloney. Finally, Stringbean Noonan squeaked, "The lunch aide said it was Joey."

There were murmurs of agreement. "Yeah, yep. Must have been Joey."

"Are you sure?" I asked. "Did anyone else see Joey start the food fight?"

Bigs moved a step closer. "If the lunch aide said it was Joey, then it was Joey." He looked around the room. "Any questions?"

I didn't say anything.

But I didn't believe it.

I knew Joey Pignattano well. We were pals. Joey Pignattano was the last guy on earth who would throw food. He'd much rather eat it. I stepped into the hallway. Suddenly, a long, bony finger pointed at me. "You."

It was Mrs. Randolph, with her sharp nose and small dark eyes.

"M-m-m-me?" I stammered.

"You're the Jones boy, right?" she said.

"Yes."

"I want you to walk this child to the nurse's office," she ordered.

"The nurse's office," I said. "What is it?"

"It's a small room with a cot and a little sink," she squawked. "But never mind that. This boy doesn't feel well."

The small, dark-haired boy was from a different second-grade classroom. His name was Ali Shrivastava. He held a hand over his eye and groaned.

"Are you okay?" I asked.

He nodded once.

 26

"Follow me, Cyclops," I said.

I met my class coming from the other direction. Ms. Gleason marched everyone back to our classroom. She looked furious.

"Where are you two going?" she snapped.

"Um, uh." I pointed at Ali. "He . . . uh . . . I'm taking him to the nurse's office."

Ms. Gleason looked at Ali.

"I've got something in my eye," he bleated.

"Make it snappy," Ms. Gleason said.

The rest of my class slowly filed past on their way to room 201. No one dared speak. The thrill of the food fight was long gone. All that was left was the shame and the punishment.

"Let's go," I whispered to Ali. We were glad to be walking in the opposite direction.

Chapter Five

Nurse Hilton

The door to the nurse's office was closed.

I tried the knob. It was locked, too.

"That's odd."

I knocked.

Ali put his ear against the door. "I hear noises," he said.

"Hello?" I called out. "Anybody home?"

Like Ali, I pressed my ear to the door.

I heard a chair scraping across the floor . . . a hushed whisper . . . a file cabinet

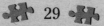

slamming shut . . . a muffled *yip yip* sound . . . and footsteps coming closer.

A young woman opened the door. "I'm sorry. Was it locked?" she asked. I had never seen her before. She was impossibly tall and thin. She had blond hair. And long legs that went all the way to the floor.

I jerked a finger at Ali. "He got something in his eye."

"I think it's pizza pie," Ali explained.

The nurse pushed out her lower lip. "Oh, dear. I'm Nurse Hilton. I'm filling in for Ms. Mosher this week. Let's take a look."

"It's *in my eye*," Ali protested. "I *can't* take a look at it."

Yip-yip, yap-yap.

I looked toward the file cabinet. "Did you hear something?"

Nurse Hilton ignored me.

"Take away your hand," the nurse said to Ali. "Don't be afraid. I may not be the regular nurse but I know how to do my job."

I glanced around the room. The desktop overflowed with stacks of folders. Some had even fallen on the floor. A travel magazine was opened to a photo of Paris. I saw lipstick and a hand mirror.

"I thought I heard a dog bark," Ali said.

The nurse looked away. "Probably outside," she said.

I got up to look out the window. "I don't see anything."

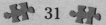

Ms. Hilton smiled tightly. "I don't hear anything, either. Must be a false alarm."

"Yeah, must be," I replied.

To be honest, I didn't really care. I was already thinking about Joey. He said he was innocent. And I believed him. But how could I prove it? I had to find out who *really* started the food fight.

I thought about Bobby and Helen's argument this morning. "We'll finish this at lunch," Bobby had said to her. I wondered if it was a threat. Or a promise. Or both.

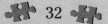

I thought about Bigs. He acted strange in the bathroom. But if he did start the food fight, I wondered if anyone would have the guts to say so. Bigs was the roughest, toughest kid in the entire second grade. Nobody messed with Bigs Maloney.

Ms. Hilton washed out Ali's eye over the sink. "He'll be fine," she said.

"Did you see how the food fight started?" I asked Ali.

"No," he said. "All I saw was a slice of pizza coming at my face."

I began the long, slow walk back to room 201. I saw Joey as I passed the main lobby. He was sitting outside the principal's office, waiting. His hands were folded on his lap. He looked scared to death.

I scribbled a secret message on a slip of paper. It was for Mila. It was in code. And it was a big mistake.

Chapter Six

No Recess

I peeked into room 201. Principal Rogers was there. Uh-oh.

He was talking quietly to the class. No one moved a muscle. No one even blinked. They just stared at him, perfectly still, like the little angels they weren't. I silently walked to my seat. I wished I was invisible.

"I am disappointed in you," Principal Rogers told the class. "You are such lucky children. I don't know that you realize it. You live in nice houses. You go to a

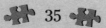

wonderful school. You have nice clothes and healthy food to eat. It's important for you to remember that not everyone in the world is so lucky. Maybe you need to start thinking about that." He paused, meeting eyes with Ms. Gleason. She nodded in agreement.

Principal Rogers continued, "I know that you are good children, but today, you were selfish."

Then he handed out the punishment: No recess.

A gasp filled the room. No recess! *Aaaaarrrgggh.*

In the confusion, I passed the secret message to Mila.

Bobby raised his hand. "Will we have recess tomorrow?"

Mr. Rogers frowned. "Not today. Not tomorrow."

"What about the day *after* tomorrow?" Solofsky asked. He was pushing his luck.

"We shall see," Principal Rogers sharply replied.

"The children have already started on their letters of apology," Ms. Gleason explained. "They are writing to the lunch aides and the cafeteria ladies."

Principal Rogers nodded, then turned to leave. He opened the door and spoke: "Theodore Jones, Mila Yeh, please meet me in the hallway." He paused. "And bring the note."

Chapter Seven

Caught!

Mila and I stood shoulder to shoulder in an empty hallway. Principal Rogers towered over us. I would have rather been a mouse staring at a fifty-pound pussycat.

He held the note in his hand:

J	O	E	Y	D	I
W	E	M	U	S	D
T	H	I	M	T	N
I	P	L	E	H	O
T	R	A	T	S	T

"Is this a code?" he asked.

"Yes."

He puzzled over the note a few more moments. "I can see the name Joey," he said. "What about the rest of it?"

I glanced sideways at Mila. She looked straight ahead.

"This isn't Mila's fault," I told Principal Rogers. "I wrote the note. I passed it to Mila. She didn't know anything about it. I'm the one who should be in trouble, not Mila."

"Okay," Principal Rogers agreed. "You are the one who is in trouble. Now tell me about this secret code."

"It's a clockwise box code," I explained. "The message is written in the shape of a box. It starts in the top left corner and goes around like a clock. It ends when you wind your way to the middle."

Principal Rogers slowly read aloud: "*Joey did not start it. We must help him.*"

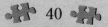

He folded the paper and placed it in his pocket. "Very clever," he said. "I see you two are still in the detective business."

Mila nodded.

Principal Rogers looked into my eyes. "Do you know who started the food fight, Theodore?"

I shook my head.

"But this note says . . ."

"I know who *didn't* start the fight," I said. "It could not have been Joey. Mrs. Randolph got the wrong guy!"

"How do you know that?" he asked.

"I just know," I answered. "It's a feeling. I know it in my heart."

Mr. Rogers rubbed his forehead. "You know that's not good enough, Jigsaw. If you want to help your friend, I need proof."

"But . . ." I began.

"I won't punish Joey today," Principal Rogers decided. "But Mrs. Randolph tells me

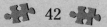 42

that Joey is to blame. I know Joey. He seems
like a nice boy. This isn't like him. But it's
Mrs. Randolph's word against his."

"Yeah, and she's a grown-up," I muttered.

Principal Rogers nodded thoughtfully.
"That's not important," he said. "What
matters is that she is an eyewitness. Mrs.
Randolph was there. She saw it with her
own eyes. She insists it was Joey."

"But she's wrong!" I pleaded.

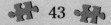

"I will give you until tomorrow to prove it," Mr. Rogers said.

"And if I can't?"

"Then," Mr. Rogers replied, "your friend Joey will be in serious trouble."

Chapter Eight

A Trick of the Eye

That same afternoon, Mila sat cross-legged on my living room floor. She softly hummed a song, *dum-dee-dum, dee-dum-dumm*.

I opened my detective journal to a new page:

The Case of the Food Fight
Client: Joey Pignattano
Suspects? Everybody!

"I don't even know where to begin!" I complained.

"Let's start at the beginning," Mila said. "We have to answer two questions: Who started the food fight? And how can we prove it?"

Those were two tough questions. I guess that's why we got paid the big bucks. "Solofsky is always a good place to start," I suggested. "When there's trouble, he's usually in the middle of it."

Mila nodded. "Bobby definitely threw food. But I didn't find one person who said he started it."

"What about Helen?" I asked. "She was arguing with Bobby this morning. She's got a bad temper. I wouldn't be surprised if she got mad and threw a handful of Jell-O."

Mila just shook her head. "Jigsaw, I talked to more than ten witnesses today. Everybody has a different story. It's crazy. Except they do have one thing in common."

"What's that?"

"No one saw who started it," Mila

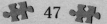

answered. "The cafeteria was like a zoo. Kids were jumping, running, screaming, laughing. Geetha Nair even told me she heard a dog barking. The truth is, no one saw Joey do a single thing."

"You are forgetting Mrs. Randolph," I reminded Mila.

Mila rocked back and forth. She sighed deeply. "What if Joey really did start the food fight?"

"Not Joey," I said. "He loves food too much. Besides, Joey told me he's innocent. And I trust him."

"You're probably right," Mila replied. "It's weird that Mrs. Randolph says Joey did it."

"Witnesses are funny," I answered with a shrug. "They can be wrong even when they are sure they are right. Sometimes two witnesses will disagree about what they saw. One might say a robber wore a mustache and a blue hat. The other might claim the

robber had a ponytail and a red beard. In the confusion, their eyes can play tricks on them."

"I guess," Mila said.

I grabbed a marker and drew a picture on a piece of paper:

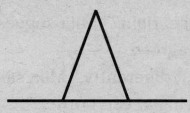

"What do you see?" I asked Mila.

She blinked. "A long triangle on top of a line."

"Yes, but what is it a picture of?"

"Um . . ." Mila nodded and petted Rags thoughtfully. "It's a sailboat on the ocean."

"Maybe," I replied. "Or maybe it's a witch's hat. Your eyes see what they want to see."

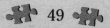

"Like an optical illusion!" Mila exclaimed. She grabbed my journal. Mila carefully drew a picture.

"It's a vase, right?" Mila suggested.

"Sure," I agreed.

"Look at it differently," Mila said. "It's two people staring at each other."

"That's sooo cool!"

"Here's another one," I offered.

I wrote these words on a piece of paper. "Read this fast," I told Mila.

A
BIRD
IN THE
THE TREE

"A bird in the tree," Mila said.

I smiled. "It gets people every time. There's an extra THE in there, but everybody skips it because they already think they know what it says."

Mila nodded. "I understand. The eye does play tricks. We both know that Mrs. Randolph is wrong. But that's not much help to Joey."

Mila was right. It was still Mrs. Randolph's word against Joey's.

"What about Bigs Maloney?" I asked.

"If Bigs started it," Mila replied, "no one will dare tell on him."

I agreed. Bigs was rough and tough. No one would cross him. You don't tattle on King Kong. The big ape might get mad.

"Bigs might be our man," I murmured.

"It would explain why no one saw how the fight started," Mila agreed. "Every witness would be afraid to talk."

Chapter Nine

A Clue

This case was making my throat dry.

"Grape juice?" I offered.

"Please," Mila answered.

I went into the kitchen, trailed by Rags. He was always underfoot, hoping for crumbs. The kitchen was just about his favorite place on earth. I came back balancing a tray of pretzel nuggets and grape juice. *WHOMP, OOF, WELP!* YIKES! I tripped over Rags. Grape juice splattered everywhere.

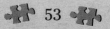

Everywhere? Well, not exactly. Mostly it flew right into Mila's face.

"Oh, Jigsaw!" Mila scolded. Grape juice dripped off her nose and chin.

"I'm sorry, Mila. I'll get you a towel. But it wasn't my fault," I protested. "I tripped over Rags! He can't stay away from food."

Moments later, there was a knock at the door. Our star witness had arrived.

"Hey, Joey," I greeted him. "Come on in."

"What happened to you?" he asked Mila. "Did you just take a shower?"

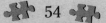

"More or less," Mila groaned.

Joey sniffed the air. "Is that perfume you're wearing?" he asked Mila.

"Yes, it's called grape juice." Mila laughed. "Jigsaw spilled it all over me!"

"It wasn't my fault," I protested. "Blame Rags. He tripped me!"

Joey smiled. But as he sank into the couch, I could see that his hopes were sinking, too.

"How are you doing?" I asked him.

"I'm toast," Joey moaned. "Put a fork in me. I'm done."

"Don't give up hope," Mila urged. "We'll find a way to help you."

Joey looked like he didn't quite believe Mila. I wasn't so sure myself.

Mila put a hand on Joey's shoulder. "I have to ask you," she said. "Did you do it?"

Joey looked her in the eye. "No," he replied.

Mila nodded. "Good answer."

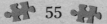

"Let's go over the food fight step-by-step," I said. "Try to remember every detail, Joey."

"I didn't see much," Joey admitted. "I was building a sculpture of the Empire State Building and —"

"What?"

"A sculpture."

"You were building a sculpture *in the cafeteria*?" I said. "I don't understand."

"Out of mashed potatoes," Joey explained. "Then I was going to eat the whole building in one bite!"

Mila rolled her eyes.

I snapped my fingers. "Maybe that's it!" I said. "Maybe Mrs. Randolph saw you with mashed potatoes in your hands!"

"Maybe," Mila said. "But that doesn't explain why Mrs. Randolph said Joey *started* the food fight."

"I know why." Joey grimaced.

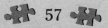

We stood staring at him. Waiting.

"She doesn't like me," Joey confessed.

"That's silly," Mila said.

"No, it's true!" Joey said. He really meant it. "She's been out to get me ever since I knocked a cactus onto her head."

A cactus!

On her head!

"What?!" Mila and I asked at the same time.

Joey ran his fingers through his hair. "It was in the waiting room at the doctor's office. She was sitting there and I was leaving. I reached for my backpack and knocked a cactus off a shelf. It landed on Mrs. Randolph's head."

"Oh, Joey," I sighed.

Joey took off his glasses and wiped them on his shirt. He squinted. "I think it hurt," he said. "I mean, she screamed a lot."

"Wait a minute," Mila said. "What doctor

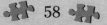

was this? Grown-ups don't go to the same doctors as kids do."

"My eye doctor," Joey said. "I had to get new glasses."

Mila suddenly grabbed my arm.

"That's it!" she exclaimed. "Mrs. Randolph wears glasses!"

"Yeah, so?" I said.

"She wasn't wearing glasses today!" Mila said.

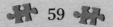

I closed my eyes and thought. I remembered Mrs. Randolph's bony finger pointing at me. Her sharp nose like a beak. Her scrawny legs. I remembered her *squinting at me through small dark eyes.*

Mila was right.

Mrs. Randolph wasn't wearing her glasses!

The eyewitness against Joey... COULDN'T SEE!

Chapter Ten

Missing Pieces

I couldn't wait to get to school in the morning. "Come on, come on," I urged the clock as I waited at the bus stop. I had a mystery to solve. There was still more work to be done.

Finally, the bus arrived. Mila slid into the seat beside me. "We know Joey didn't start the food fight," I said to her. "I'm sure that Principal Rogers will agree that Mrs. Randolph isn't a good witness without her glasses."

"We did it, Jigsaw," Mila said with a broad smile. "We saved Joey."

"Still," I added, "we can't stop now. The puzzle isn't finished. There are missing pieces."

"Bigs Maloney," Mila whispered.

I glanced backward. Bigs was sitting a few rows behind us.

Yes, I thought, *Bigs Maloney.* I had a hunch he was involved in the food fight from the

beginning. If no one would tell on him, there was only one chance left.

"I'm going to see if I can make Bigs confess," I told Mila.

Her eyes widened. "How are you going to do that?"

"I'm going to have to squeeze him," I said.

"What if Bigs squeezes back?"

"I'm a detective," I told Mila. "Danger is part of the job. But don't worry. I'll be careful."

I gazed out the window as the bus wound its way through town. A mystery is like a jigsaw puzzle. And I could never walk away from an unfinished puzzle. I had to have every piece in place.

Geetha Nair climbed on the bus at the next stop. I suddenly slapped my head.

"I can't believe it," I said out loud. "Geetha! Yes, yes, it must be!"

"Jigsaw? What are you talking about?" Mila asked.

 63

"Yesterday you told me that Geetha heard a dog barking in the cafeteria," I said to Mila excitedly.

"She *thought* she heard a dog," Mila said. "But that's impossible. Dogs aren't allowed in school. And people would have seen it."

I remembered tripping over Rags yesterday. "*He can't stay away from food*," I had told Mila. That's true for most dogs.

I leaped off the bus the moment it pulled

into the school parking lot. "Quick, come with me," I said to Mila.

"Where are we going?" she asked.

"The nurse's office," I answered. "I'll explain everything when we get there."

The door to the office was closed. I didn't try the knob. Instead, I placed a finger to my lips. I leaned my ear against the door and listened. Someone was inside. It was Nurse Hilton.

Her voice was a high-pitched whisper. I could barely make out the words. "You are my wittle sweet 'ums, my wittle sweetie pie. Yes you are, yes you are!"

I knocked sharply on the door. I hoped it would startle her.

Yip-yap.

"Shhhh."

My plan worked.

A file cabinet slid open, then closed. In a moment, Nurse Hilton opened the door. She smiled stiffly at us. "Can I help you?"

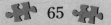 65

"We need to talk," I said.

Nurse Hilton raised her perfect blond eyebrows. "Oh? Talk about what?"

"About the dog you've been hiding in your file cabinet," I replied.

Nurse Hilton instantly pulled us into the room.

And locked the door.

Chapter Eleven
Tripping Up Bigs

Tinkerbell weighed two pounds. She was six inches tall, with pointy ears that stood straight up. She had a sharp nose and large round eyes.

Tinkerbell was a Chihuahua. A tiny dog that had been hiding in a file cabinet in the nurse's office for the past three days.

Mila dropped to her knees and cooed. It was love at first sight. "She's soooo *cute!*"

"I know it's against the rules," Nurse Hilton admitted. "But I couldn't leave her home alone. I just couldn't do it."

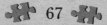

I glanced around the office. The files were still stacked on the desk. It was an early clue that I had missed. Ms. Hilton had to empty the file cabinet to make room for Tinkerbell!

"Tinkerbell escaped yesterday, didn't she?" I asked Nurse Hilton.

She bit her lip. And nodded yes.

"Dogs come in all sizes," I said. "My dog is extra large. But big or small, they all love food."

Mila stopped petting Tinkerbell long enough to listen. "What are you saying, Jigsaw?" she asked.

"Did Tinkerbell run into the cafeteria yesterday?" I asked Nurse Hilton. "Before you answer, you should know that I have a witness who heard barking."

Again, Nurse Hilton nodded. "Please don't tell on me," she pleaded. "They'll never hire me as a substitute nurse again."

"You can't keep that dog here," I said.

"I know," Nurse Hilton admitted.

"Did you see Tinkerbell run into the cafeteria yesterday?" I asked.

"I followed her," the nurse answered. "Chihuahuas are so fast and lively. She got away from me . . ."

". . . and headed straight for the meatballs," I added.

"Tinkerbell almost got stepped on," Nurse Hilton said. "A tall boy with large feet tripped over her."

"Bigs Maloney!" Mila said.

"Yes, Bigs Maloney," I echoed. "That's how the food fight started, isn't it? It wasn't Bigs Maloney's fault. He tripped over a tiny dog and spilled his food."

Mila smiled wide. "That's when the food started flying!" she exclaimed. "Nobody started the food fight! No one is to blame. Not really, anyway."

I tilted my head from side to side. I eyed Nurse Hilton. I reached down to pet

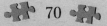

Tinkerbell, who snapped at me with sharp teeth. *Grrrrr.*

"No," I said. "There isn't *one* person to blame for the food fight. Except I think we are *all* to blame."

"Well, I've been thinking about that," Mila said. "I even talked to a few of the girls last night. We have an idea. . . ."

An hour later, Mila was standing in front of our classroom. Beside her stood Kim

Lewis, Geetha Nair, and Danika Starling. Ms. Gleason watched from her desk.

"We've been doing a lot of thinking," Danika said.

"We know we were wrong for wasting good food yesterday," Kim added.

"Very, very wrong," Geetha said in a shy whisper. She stared at her feet while she spoke, not daring to look anyone in the eye.

"We're sorry," Mila continued. "And we want to do something that will help make it

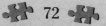

right." She looked nervously around the classroom.

"We want to show that we care about more than just ourselves," Danika added. "So we were thinking . . ."

Chapter Twelve

Car Wash

The next Saturday morning, everyone from the second grade met in the school parking lot.

We had buckets of water, soap, sponges, and plenty of rags.

Out front we set up a huge sign. It read:

CHARITY CAR WASH

A long row of cars was already lined up.

"We're going to make a bundle!" Eddie Becker exclaimed.

"Yes, and it's all going to children in need," Ms. Gleason said.

At the other end of the parking lot, some kids were collecting cans of food. We were going to give those away, too.

"Uh-oh," groaned Joey Pignattano. "Look."

Mrs. Randolph pulled up in a speedy red roadster. Hers was the next car in line.

I noticed that she wore a new pair of silver eyeglasses.

Mrs. Randolph rolled down her window. She smiled at Joey. "I'm sorry about the other day," she said. "I was wrong and I apologize."

Joey smiled. "Well, I guess I apologize, too. I should be more careful around cactuses."

Mrs. Randolph tilted back her head

and laughed, loud and long. Joey laughed, too. Who could blame them? Hey, it was funny.

The Case of the Food Fight was solved. Every piece of the puzzle was in its place. Joey wasn't in trouble. We learned that Bigs Maloney didn't start the fight after all.

CHARITY
CAR WASH

The whole mess began because of a little dog named Tinkerbell.

As for Nurse Hilton, I never saw her again.

Which was too bad.

She was good for business.

About the Author

James Preller often draws upon his own life as a basis for his Jigsaw Jones books. Like Jigsaw, James Preller has a slobbering, sock-eating dog. Like Jigsaw, James was the youngest in a large family. His older brothers called him Worm and worse — yeesh! And so do Jigsaw's!

James and Jigsaw both love jigsaw puzzles, baseball, grape juice, and mysteries! But even though Jigsaw and James have so much in common, they are not the same person.

Unlike Jigsaw, James Preller is the author of more than 80 books for children, including *The Big Book of Picture-Book Authors & Illustrators; Wake Me in Spring; Hiccups for Elephant;* and *Cardinal & Sunflower*. He lives in Delmar, New York, with his wife, Lisa, three kids —Nicholas, Gavin, and Maggie — his cat, Blue, and his dog, Seamus.

Mysteries are like jigsaw puzzles—you've got to look at all the pieces to solve the case!

0-590-69125-2	#1: The Case of Hermie the Missing Hamster	$3.99 US
0-590-69126-0	#2: The Case of the Christmas Snowman	$3.99 US
0-590-69127-9	#3: The Case of the Secret Valentine	$3.99 US
0-590-69129-5	#4: The Case of the Spooky Sleepover	$3.99 US
0-439-08083-5	#5: The Case of the Stolen Baseball Cards	$3.99 US
0-439-08094-0	#6: The Case of the Mummy Mystery	$3.99 US
0-439-11426-8	#7: The Case of the Runaway Dog	$3.99 US
0-439-11427-6	#8: The Case of the Great Sled Race	$3.99 US
0-439-11428-4	#9: The Case of the Stinky Science Project	$3.99 US
0-439-11429-2	#10: The Case of the Ghostwriter	$3.99 US
0-439-18473-8	#11: The Case of the Marshmallow Monster	$3.99 US
0-439-18474-6	#12: The Case of the Class Clown	$3.99 US
0-439-18476-2	#13: The Case of the Detective in Disguise	$3.99 US
0-439-18477-0	#14: The Case of the Bicycle Bandit	$3.99 US
0-439-30637-X	#15: The Case of the Haunted Scarecrow	$3.99 US
0-439-30638-8	#16: The Case of the Sneaker Sneak	$3.99 US
0-439-30639-6	#17: The Case of the Disappearing Dinosaur	$3.99 US
0-439-30640-X	#18: The Case of the Bear Scare	$3.99 US
0-439-42628-6	#19: The Case of the Golden Key	$3.99 US
0-439-42630-8	#20: The Case of the Race Against Time	$3.99 US
0-439-42631-6	#21: The Case of the Rainy Day Mystery	$3.99 US
0-439-55995-2	#22: The Case of the Best Pet Ever	$3.99 US
0-439-55996-0	#23: The Case of the Perfect Prank	$3.99 US
0-439-55998-7	#24: The Case of the Glow-in-the-Dark Ghost	$3.99 US
0-439-66165-X	#25: The Case of the Vanishing Painting	$3.99 US
0-439-67804-8	#26: The Case of the Double Trouble Detectives	$3.99 US
0-439-67805-6	#27: The Case of the Frog Jumping Contest	$3.99 US
0-439-67807-2	#28: The Case of the Food Fight	$3.99 US

Super Specials

0-439-30931-X	#1: The Case of the Buried Treasure	$3.99 US
0-439-42629-4	#2: The Case of the Million-Dollar Mystery	$3.99 US
0-439-55997-9	#3: The Case of the Missing Falcon	$3.99 US

THE SECRETS OF DROON

By Tony Abbott

Under the stairs, a magical world awaits you!

$3.99 each!

- ☐ 0-590-10839-5   #1: The Hidden Stairs and the Magic Carpet
- ☐ 0-590-10841-7   #2: Journey to the Volcano Palace
- ☐ 0-590-10840-9   #3: The Mysterious Island
- ☐ 0-590-10842-5   #4: City in the Clouds
- ☐ 0-590-10843-3   #5: The Great Ice Battle
- ☐ 0-590-10844-1   #6: The Sleeping Giant of Goll
- ☐ 0-439-18297-2   #7: Into the Land of the Lost
- ☐ 0-439-18298-0   #8: The Golden Wasp
- ☐ 0-439-20772-X   #9: The Tower of the Elf King
- ☐ 0-439-20784-3   #10: Quest for the Queen
- ☐ 0-439-20785-1   #11: The Hawk Bandits of Tarkoom
- ☐ 0-439-20786-X   #12: Under the Serpent Sea
- ☐ 0-439-30606-X   #13: The Mask of Maliban
- ☐ 0-439-30607-8   #14: Voyage of the *Jaffa Wind*
- ☐ 0-439-30608-6   #15: The Moon Scroll
- ☐ 0-439-30609-4   #16: The Knights of Silversnow
- ☐ 0-439-42078-4   #17: Dream Thief
- ☐ 0-439-42079-2   #18: Search for the Dragon Ship
- ☐ 0-439-42080-6   #19: The Coiled Viper
- ☐ 0-439-56040-3   #20: In the Ice Caves of Krog
- ☐ 0-439-56043-8   #21: Flight of the Genie
- ☐ 0-439-56048-9   #22: The Isle of Mists
- ☐ 0-439-66157-9   #23: The Fortress of the Treasure Queen
- ☐ 0-439-66158-7   #24: The Race to Doobesh
- ☐ 0-439-67173-6   #25: The Riddle of Zorfendorf Castle
- ☐ 0-439-42077-6   Special Edition #1: The Magic Escapes $5.99
- ☐ 0-439-56049-7   Special Edition #2: Wizard or Witch? $5.99

Available Wherever You Buy Books or Use This Order Form

scholastic.com/droon   📖 **SCHOLASTIC**

SODBL0505

Get your kicks from

THE BLACK BELT CLUB

THE BLACK BELT CLUB
Seven Wheels of Power
by **DAWN BARNES**
ILLUSTRATED BY BERNARD CHANG

0-439-63936-0 • $4.99 U.S.

Join karate students Max, Maia, Antonio, and Jamie as they take on a terrible menace in their first secret martial-arts mission. Will these black belts find the strength and skill to battle danger and overcome evil? It will require courage, focus, and teamwork. But no matter what happens, these kids always try their best and never, ever give up!

Available wherever books are sold
www.theblackbeltclub.com
www.scholastic.com/blackbeltclub

THE BLUE SKY PRESS

SCHOLASTIC and associated logos are trademarks and/or registered trademarks of Scholastic Inc.

BBCT